W9-BGL-110

The Great
FOURTH GRADE
DISASTER

by Janet Adele Bloss

illustrated by Don Robison

Published by Willowisp Press, Inc.
401 E. Wilson Bridge Road, Worthington, Ohio 43085

Copyright © 1988 by Willowisp Press, Inc.

All rights reserved. No portion of this book may be reproduced,
stored in a retrieval system, or transmitted, in any form or by any
means, electronic, mechanical, photocopying, recording, or other-
wise without prior written permission from the publisher.

Printed in the United States of America

10 9 8 7 6 5 4 3 2 1

ISBN 0-87406-278-0

One

"STOP! Stop!" yelled Ms. Angelvine. "We're missing someone! There should be twenty-*five* children on board. Who's missing?"

The bus driver pulled over to the side of the road. As I finished tying my left shoe, I wondered who could be missing. Then I started on the right shoe. Whoever it was would be pretty sorry if he or she missed our field trip today. We were going to visit "IST," the Institute of Science and Technology. After a month of waiting, we were actually on our way!

My head almost touched the floor as I leaned over, tugging at my shoelaces. They were always coming untied, and I didn't want to trip over them. I planned to get through the day without being called a klutz by Creepy Craig Fuller.

"Fawn Forrester! Has anyone seen her?" called Ms. Angelvine. "Oh, dear, I thought I saw her get on the bus. Fawn?"

Bev nudged me with her elbow.

When I realized that the missing person was *me,* I quickly tried to sit up in my seat. "Here I am, Ms. OUCH!" I banged my head on the top of the seat before me.

All of my classmates on the bus started laughing. Bobby McDonald looked like he would split from laughter. But Ms. Angelvine just looked relieved.

The bus driver turned the bus back onto the road, and we began our journey once again. Simmons Elementary School disappeared behind us. We passed houses, then barns, then open fields. It wasn't long before our bus left the small town of Simmons. It headed down the highway toward Frankfort, the state capital.

Everyone was pretty excited. We all talked and

laughed and squirmed in our seats.

Every year the fourth-graders get to choose if they want to go on a field trip to the zoo or IST. We chose IST because everyone thought that all the science things that Ms. Angelvine described would be neat. We were going to see a planetarium, visit a coal mine, and go to one exhibit that lets people freeze their shadows on a screen.

The lucky kids got to sit by the windows. I was lucky because my seatmate was Bev Miller, my best friend. She let me have the window seat. It's just like Bev to do that. She's always nice to other people.

Our fourth-grade teacher, Ms. Angelvine, sat at the front of the bus. We were supposed to meet our chaperone—"somebody who's special" said our teacher—at IST.

Ms. Angelvine is a pretty neat teacher. She hardly ever gets angry at us. She also lets us do a lot of extra fun things as rewards for hard work. Our favorite thing is sports. This grading period we got to have soccer intramurals because everyone had done super science projects.

I leaned back into my seat and stared out the window. It seemed like the bus trip was taking forever. As our bus crossed a bridge, I looked at the reflection it made in the river below. Then I thought about the intramurals. Our class was divided into two teams: the Ground Hoggers and the Turkey Busters. I was elected the captain of the Ground Hoggers because I'm a pretty good athlete. But, unfortunately, my great archenemy, Craig Fuller, was chosen to be captain of the Turkey Busters. (Creepy Craig hasn't stopped picking on me since third grade.) My team won the last game, and that really burned Craig up. Our final game is next week, and that will decide the champs—who, of course, will be the Ground Hoggers.

"Fifteen miles to go," said Bev. "That's what the sign said. Oh, Fawn, I'm so excited!"

Soon, heavy traffic surrounded our bus. Cars zipped by us. The highway changed from two to four lanes. We could see tall buildings from our windows. Our bus left the highway for the downtown streets.

Traffic lights blinked at street corners, and people thronged the sidewalks. Our driver threaded his way to a tall, modern building with glass windows that shone like silver. He pulled to the curb in front and parked.

"We're here," announced Ms. Angelvine as she stood up. "Now, everyone behave. You will all stay right by me in the lobby until we're ready to go on the exhibits. I have some very important announcements to make inside."

Bev stepped out into the aisle. I started to follow her, but Craig jumped out in front of me. "Beauty before beast," he said.

"I'm not the beast," I shot back. I followed him along the aisle and down the steps.

The whole fourth-grade class gathered around Ms. Angelvine in the lobby.

"Wow," murmured Cheryl Anderson. "It's so-o-o-o big!"

"Hey, klutz," Craig said behind me. "Did you sit in something on the bus? What's all over your pants?"

"Oh, no!" I craned my neck over my shoulder. Hoisting up my sweater, I inspected my bottom. The back of my jeans looked just fine. I straightened my sweater and glared back at Craig.

Craig huddled together with two of his friends (Turkey Busters, of course). They giggled and pointed at me. "I made her look," laughed Craig.

"She looked! She looked!" giggled the others.

"Just ignore them," Bev advised.

In spite of Bev's advice, I felt myself becoming angry. Craig and his friends were still laughing at me. It's pretty hard to ignore creeps when they make fun of you.

Two

MS. Angelvine cleared her throat and clapped her hands together. "Class! May I please have your attention?"

Everyone settled down but Craig. "Craig Fuller!" she called. "Please be quiet. Thank you."

I couldn't help but smile. Craig glanced at me, crossed his eyes, then turned to Ms. Angelvine.

"Class," began Ms. Angelvine, "I want to remind you that we are guests of the Institute of Science and Technology today. Please behave accordingly."

Suddenly Ms. Angelvine's face lit up and she waved across the lobby. We all turned and saw a lady wave back as she came to join our group.

"Hello!" said our teacher to the white-haired lady. "Children, I am very happy to introduce Mrs. Underhill to you. She has kindly offered to assist as chaperone for your trip today. Mrs. Underhill is a pretty special person to me . . . she was *my* teacher when I was in fourth grade."

The two women looked at each other and smiled.

"As you may guess," continued Ms. Angelvine, "Mrs. Underhill is retired now."

Mrs. Underhill winked at all of us. She was a tiny lady, and she had a back as straight as an arrow. She wore a plain, dark blue dress with a pretty brooch at her neck. It had black and diamondlike stones in it, and it was in the shape of a butterfly.

"I'm very happy to be here today," said Mrs. Underhill. "It's been a while since I've been around young ladies and gentlemen your age. I wonder if you can behave better than your teacher's class did when they went someplace special."

We all laughed, especially because Ms. Angelvine was laughing.

Mrs. Underhill continued, "Well, I certainly hope so, because I think I'm too old to paddle someone."

As everyone groaned, I whispered to Bev, "Now I know why Ms. Angelvine is my favorite teacher!" I thought it was pretty neat to have our teacher's teacher along.

Ms. Angelvine thanked Mrs. Underhill for coming to help and then continued. "Now, everyone listen up. Let's see which team can show the best behavior today. Will it be the Turkey Busters or the Ground Hoggers?"

We all almost started to cheer for our own team, but the two teachers held up their hands for silence before anybody could make any noise.

"Remember," said Ms. Angelvine, "other people are here today, too. Let's all represent Simmons Elementary School to the best of our ability."

Then she asked us to make sure we all had our

IST tickets with us. I checked my pocket to make sure that my little orange ticket was there.

"Who remembers why we have to hang on to our tickets?" asked Ms. Angelvine.

Megan MacIntosh raised her hand. "So we can prove we paid for our lunch and in case we get lost," she promptly answered.

"Right!" said Ms. Angelvine. She looked at her watch. "But nobody will get lost today because you're all fourth-graders who know how to stick together. Okay, kids. Look around the lobby for about five minutes. I'll go and find our tour guide."

We all started to look around.

"Wow!" I exclaimed to Bev. "It's huge!"

The lobby was bigger than the Simmons' gymnasium. The ceiling looked like it was three floors high. Silk balloons and colorful paper kites hung by wires from the rafters. Everywhere I looked there was something interesting: glass cases containing beautiful crystals, a pool of water covered by lily pads, and even a huge space capsule! I hadn't dreamed that IST would be that neat!

"Okay, class. Please follow me," said Ms. Angelvine, clapping her hands together.

We followed our teacher and Mrs. Underhill to a large exhibit behind a velvet rope. An IST worker in a white cotton coat and a blue badge stood beside the display. "Welcome to IST!" she said cheerily. "I'm Linda, your guide. Are you all glad to be here?"

"YES!" we shouted.

"Well, IST is pleased to have your class visit, too. This first exhibit I want to show you is interesting because it was made by students your age. Each month IST allows a class of schoolchildren who have a neat idea for a display to put one up in the lobby. Perhaps you'd like to think of one."

"Can we?" we all asked Ms. Angelvine at once.

She smiled at us. "Well," she said, "we'll talk about it at the end of our trip."

Linda gestured at a display behind her. A sea of black dominoes spread across the floor.

"What are they for?" asked Bev.

Linda explained. "This idea was thought up by students from Douglas Alternative Elementary School. After experimenting with these dominoes in their gymnasium, the Douglas children made an estimate of how long it would take for all of these dominoes to fall. They counted the total number of dominoes and tried to make sure that each one they placed was the width of another domino. Also, we're supposed to be able to see a surprise message when they all fall down. All those dominoes should fall over just because the first one gets gently knocked down."

"When will that happen?" asked Jim Hunter. Jim loved neat things like this.

"This Saturday at noon," answered Linda.

"I want to see it!" several in the class exclaimed.

"Maybe some of you can talk your parents into being here for the big event. Believe it or not, the Douglas kids used 4,236 dominoes to make this exhibit!"

"Wow!" I breathed. "I wonder what the message says."

"Let me see," said Craig. He tried to shove past me but I stood my ground by the velvet rope.

"You make a better wall than a window," complained Craig. "I can't see anything."

Nobody around me seemed to notice that Craig was shoving. Probably that was because I was the only one he was shoving. I felt myself getting angry.

"Come on," said Craig. "Move over, turkey. You're blocking the view." He began pushing even harder.

That did it. I pushed Craig back with my right arm. I used all the power I had, and he went stumbling backward. But then I lost my own balance. I began to fall, and my left arm thrashed around wildly as I searched for something to hold onto. I grabbed at the velvet rope.

One of the metal stands that held the rope up tottered and then crashed to the floor. I fell on

top. Bev's eyes went wide open with shock and everybody gasped. And then I heard the sound of dominoes rapidly toppling over.

Three

"OH, dear!" exclaimed Linda. She stared at me where I lay, then knelt down near me. "Are you all right?" she asked.

"Y-yes, Ma'am," I said sadly.

I felt horrible. A crowd of people gathered around my class. Some looked like they felt sorry for me. Some of them asked, "What happened?" Ms. Angelvine stood with her hand covering her forehead.

Another IST worker came running over. You can tell who they are because they all wear white coats and blue badges. The IST man stared at the sprawling heap of tiles in the display area. He, too, asked, "What happened?"

Craig pointed at me and said, "That klutz knocked over the dominoes."

"Now, Craig," interrupted Ms. Angelvine. "I don't think we need to blame anyone for this. I'm sure that Fawn feels badly enough." Then she apologized to the IST workers and promised that her class would be more careful.

My class stared at me. Some giggled. Some looked embarrassed or mad, but I wasn't sure. But the stares of complete strangers were worse. I decided my new goal in life was to turn into a domino.

I stood and looked at the scattered mess. Most of the dominoes had flipped to show their colored sides. The message said:

WELCOME TO IST

"Welcome to IST!" murmured Linda. Clearing her throat, she smiled and said, "Well, we've certainly begun the day with some excitement, haven't we?"

I sheepishly uttered, "I'm so sorry."

Mrs. Underhill's hand patted my back. "I just bet that this young lady will be a little more careful from now on."

"I just hope we don't all get kicked out of here because of Fawn." Ms. Angelvine shot Craig a stern glance when he said that.

"I don't know what happened, but there will be no more roughhousing. Is that clear?" she said in a very serious tone. Then Ms. Angelvine turned to Linda. "Is there anything we can do—maybe rebuild the exhibit?"

"Oh, no," assured Linda. "I think the other children will understand. We'll handle it from our office."

I could tell that Ms. Angelvine was anxious to leave the scene of the crime. Bev gave me her sympathetic look. Everyone breathed a sigh of relief when Linda suggested we move on to the coal mine exhibit.

On our way there, we stopped and admired an old-fashioned fire engine.

Linda led us down a long stairway into a dark basement. Some of the kids started making spooky ghost noises.

We could hardly see a thing until an IST man in a white coat appeared, saying, "Grab yourself a lamp helmet, boys and girls. They're on the shelf." He pointed a flashlight at a row of mining hardhats with little lights on the front. I took one for myself and handed one to Bev. I switched on the light. It was neat because suddenly I could see a wall of shining, black coal in front of me.

The IST man explained that we were in a coal mine made to look like an authentic mine from 1890. He showed us a big wire box in the corner. "That," he said, "is a 'man cage.' It's the sort of elevator that they used back then. And over here," he said pointing, "is the 'man car.' That's how miners got from one end of the mine to the other. You, boys and girls, will ride that up to the next floor."

"It looks like a roller coaster," someone said.

"It *is* like a roller coaster," the IST man

agreed. "But it doesn't move as fast."

I inspected the man car. It was a string of two-seater cars sitting on a track that ran through the center of the tunnel. It really looked like fun.

Bev raised her hand.

"Yes?" The man pointed to Bev.

"Why is there a bird down here?" she asked.

I hadn't noticed it before. But in the corner of the mine was a little cage. A tiny yellow canary chirped and hopped on its wooden perch.

"Miners had to worry about oxygen levels in the mines," said the IST man. "Mining was—and still is—a dangerous occupation. But miners today have much more sophisticated safety measures. A lack of oxygen has always been a hazard for those who have worked so deep in the earth. Does anyone here think they know why the canary would be crucial to the miners' lives?"

Lots of us, including me, raised our hands and cried, "Ooh! Ooh!" hoping he would call on us.

Marsha Bryson answered. "The canary would stop chirping if it couldn't breathe anymore."

"Exactly right!" said the IST man.

Linda added, "Actually, oxygen would already be at a dangerously low level if the canary died. The miners kept an eye on the canary because if oxygen just started to get low, the canary would act funny. Then they would know that they needed to hightail it out of that mine."

"There must not be enough oxygen in our school," said Craig. "I've noticed Fawn Forrester acting pretty weird lately."

The class howled with laughter. I turned around to face Craig, but Bev nudged my elbow when she saw my jaws clench.

"Ignore him," she whispered.

Bev was right. I held my temper. I was glad I did, too, because I noticed Ms. Angelvine was looking at us.

Four

"MY father worked in a coal mine before we moved from Pennsylvania when I was a girl," Mrs. Underhill was saying. "It's very true that miners lived lives of peril."

We all turned, and our lamp helmets shined right onto Mrs. Underhill's butterfly brooch.

"Did your father ever get hurt?" asked Laurie Chester.

"Thankfully, no," answered Mrs. Underhill. "But one time part of a mine collapsed when he and six other men were in it. All the families waited for about three hours at the entrance, hoping they'd come out safely. We really cheered and cried for joy when they did!"

I thought about what that must have been like. I tried imagining Mrs. Underhill as a little girl, waiting and scared to death.

"Are those real diamonds?" asked Jim Hunt, pointing to the butterfly.

"No," said the elderly woman as she touched the pin at her neck. "Those shiny things that look like diamonds are only rhinestones. Rhinestones are made of polished glass."

"Are those black stones made out of coal?" asked Megan MacIntosh.

"No," said Mrs. Underhill again, smiling. "But they certainly do look like they are." Then she turned to the IST man and asked him if he knew anything about "jet."

"Yes," he said. "Although coal is shiny black, it isn't often used for jewelry. Miners did make objects out of coal, though—like ashtrays and animal carvings. What this lady has in her brooch is something called 'jet.' Jet is polished lignite, a type of rock."

Some kids gathered around Mrs. Underhill to

examine her pin. She let them rub their fingers on the jet and rhinestone.

Then Linda spoke up. "Something you may find hard to believe is that real diamonds start out as coal. But only nature can make genuine diamonds, and that process takes thousands of years. Diamonds are not only beautiful but they are indestructible. That's why they're so expensive. That's also why they're a symbol for love."

The IST man added, "You can make coal into diamonds if you have the right equipment."

"You can?" someone exclaimed. "We're rich! Can we take some coal home with us?"

Some kids (including Creepy Craig) grabbed pieces of coal off the floor.

"Stop!" yelled Ms. Angelvine. "Children, the coal is not to be taken out of here! Please have some manners!"

"But we want to make diamonds," said Steve Munroe.

"You would need extremely high heat and pressure to change coal into diamonds," Linda said.

"And so far mankind can only make very tiny diamonds—much, much smaller than the ones made by nature." She brushed her hand across her forehead.

I wondered if we were the worst class she'd ever had.

Kids moaned as dreams of diamond-making disappeared. Then the IST man pointed out where some shovels were. "Why don't you kids try shoveling some coal? I think that then you'll *really* appreciate the work of a miner."

"I'll wait for you on the train," Bev said to me. "I don't want to shovel."

"Okay. I'll be there in a minute." I grabbed a shovel and lifted a small pile of coal.

"Why don't you join her?" asked Craig. He aimed his lamp helmet right into my face. "This coal shoveling is too hard for girls. You should let the boys do it."

"Get out of my way, wimp," I said, turning to the task before me. I scooted my shovel under a larger pile of coal. It weighed about a ton. But I wasn't about to let Craig see me fail. With all my might, I lifted the coal.

I picked up another shovelful and added it to my pile. "What's the matter, Craig?" I asked. "Did your muscles have a blowout?" Beads of sweat formed on my forehead as I continued to shovel coal.

"I can shovel more than you any day," taunted Craig. "It's just that I'd rather shovel from the real thing, not from this baby pile you found."

"What do you mean?"

"There's a mountain of coal around the corner from here," Craig informed me. "We can have a race if we go over there. Unless, of course, you're chicken."

I balanced my shovel on my shoulder. "Lead the way," I offered. "I want to prove who's the best."

"Oh, no . . . after YOU." Craig stuck his tongue out at me.

We walked away from where the rest of the class was digging and talking. Past a curve in the

wall, we found ourselves in a darker room away from the main tunnel. A giant heap of black coal reached up to the ceiling.

Craig forced his shovel into a mound. I did the same. "READY—SET—GO!" he shouted.

Furiously we shoveled. Neither of us said a word because this was truly war. It was an official "who-can-shovel-the-most-coal" war. We each shoveled from the hill, building our own piles. Steadily they grew. I kept my eye on Craig's pile. Mine was a little larger, but it looked like he was going to catch up with me. Gritting my teeth, I shoveled faster, wondering if fourth graders could have heart attacks.

WHOOOOOOOOooooo! WwwwwhOOOOOO!

Craig and I froze.

CHUGGA-CHUGGA-CHUGGA-Chugga-chugga woooooooooo!

"Oh, no!" I yelled. I ran from the coal room into the main tunnel. The train's taillights were specks of red in the distance. They disappeared around a bend in the tracks. All I saw were empty tracks, piles of coal, and a small sparkle from the ground.

Craig dropped his shovel. "Now you've really done it. Ms. Angelvine is going to kill us!"

"*I've* done it?" I cried. "This would never have happened if you didn't have to prove you're such a hot shot!"

"You're the one who thinks you're a hot shot!" said Craig.

"I do not!"

Our helmet lamps shined directly into each other's eyes. We were surrounded by darkness and silence. Not one IST person was near. I couldn't believe it. Not only was I left behind in a dark, cold cave, but I was stranded with the worst, nerdiest, creepiest creep in the world— Craig Fuller!

"What'll we do now, Miss Hot Shot?" muttered Craig.

I looked around. The train track stretched into a dark tunnel. It might not be safe to walk down there. How would we ever find our class? Should we wait until someone found us? Should we go back up the stairs to where we started? Suddenly, I saw something that gave me hope. I walked toward it.

"Where are you going?" asked Craig.

"Through that door," I said, pointing. A metal door was at the bottom of the stairs.

"But you don't know where it leads," said Craig. "What if it gets us *more* lost?"

"What if it doesn't?" I said with determination.

My hand rested on the doorknob. For some reason I pictured a snake pit on the other side. Should I open the door? Did I have the guts?

Five

"CHICKEN," Craig said.

That did it. Taking a deep breath, I turned the knob and pushed forward.

I found myself standing in the middle of a stage with a man who wore a white coat and a blue IST badge. He stared at Craig and me in surprise. "Well, ladies and gentlemen," he said, "it looks like we found our volunteers."

A large group of people surrounding the stage began laughing. As they did, I thought about running back through the door into the coal mine. But Craig was right behind me.

"Here you go, young man," the IST man said. He handed Craig a mirror.

Craig looked at it and was actually nerdy enough to say, "Hmmmm. I get better-looking every day."

Again the crowd laughed. I saw a few girls about my age start to giggle and whisper to each other.

"Now, young lady," said the scientist, "would you just place your hands, like so, on the electrostatic generator?"

"The what?" I asked. I stared at a silver dome on top of a narrow table. The silver part was the size of a soccer ball.

"Just place your hands on the top," encouraged the man. "This won't hurt a bit."

I wasn't sure if I should be grateful or terrified.

"Please don't remove your hands from the generator—something very interesting will happen," he said, looking toward the audience.

Wonderful, I thought to myself sarcastically.

"I'll do it if she's too scared," offered Craig.

"Oh, that's okay," I said out loud, smiling. I gave Craig a dirty look. Then I put my hand on top of the silver dome. Relief. Nothing happened. No shocks. No bolts of lightning flew out of my ears.

The IST man turned a dial and a low humming noise came from the generator. There still wasn't any pain, so I wasn't worried. That is, I wasn't worried until everyone began pointing at me and laughing. I looked down at my feet, but they looked the same as usual. I glanced over my shoulder to make sure Craig wasn't making faces behind my back. But he just stared back at me as if I had six eyeballs.

"What's going on?" I asked.

Craig walked in front of me and held up the mirror so I could see myself. I couldn't believe it!

Usually my hair just falls straight down to my shoulders. But now it was all sticking straight out! I looked like a dandelion right before you make a wish and blow on it.

Craig turned to the audience and said, "Ladies and gentlemen, I present the winner of the Miss Porcupine contest!"

Laughter erupted from the audience. I would have socked Craig, except that I didn't dare take my hands off of the generator. At last, the scientist turned the dial and the hum died away. Craig held the mirror in front of me so I could watch my hair fall back into place. I took my hands away from the silver dome and hurried to the side of the stage where the exit was.

The IST man called after me, "Would you like to know what just happened to you?"

I knew what just happened to me, all right. I just looked like a major fool for the second time that day—in front of lots of people, of course.

"No, thanks. I'm supposed to meet somebody," I politely replied. I strode toward the door at the back of the room. The scientist started talking about static electricity.

Craig hurried after me.

As soon as we were outside, Craig laughed and pointed a finger at me. "Gee, Fawn, why did you leave in such a hurry?"

I glared at him. "Oh, you know—standing on a

stage and being laughed at gets *so* boring after a while." I started walking toward an area full of shops. Overhead a sign pronounced, "Ye Olde Time Village."

Craig continued to follow me. He also continued to laugh at me, telling me what a great guinea pig I was and how many millions of dollars my parents could make if I donated my body to science.

"Listen, Craig," I hissed, "you've gotten me into big trouble twice today. Do you think you could activate your brain cell and help me figure out a way to find our class?"

"*I* got *you* into trouble?" asked Craig in disbelief. He opened his mouth to argue some more, but I continued.

"We've got to find somebody who works here who can help us get back to Ms. Angelvine. Let's go over there." I pointed over to Ye Olde Time Village.

"Wait," Craig insisted. "If we try to find the end of the coal tunnel, maybe we can join the class without anybody noticing us. Then *I* won't get into trouble because of *you*."

I couldn't believe my ears. "You creep! You're the one who got us lost. Anyway, they have to know we're missing by now."

"How do you know?" asked Craig.

I looked at him. Maybe he actually had *two* brain cells. Maybe we could find the class easily. Maybe no one had noticed we were left behind. Maybe—

"WOULD FAWN FORRESTER AND CRAIG FULLER PLEASE MEET MRS. UNDERHILL AT THE INFORMATION BOOTH IN THE LOBBY IMMEDIATELY! WOULD FAWN FORRESTER AND CRAIG FULLER PLEASE REPORT TO THE INFORMATION BOOTH IN THE LOBBY IMMEDIATELY!"

"Oh, great!" I groaned. "So much for your brilliant suggestion. Let's go find someone who can tell us how to get to the lobby," I said as I headed toward Ye Olde Time Village.

"No, let's go over here," said Craig, and he started to run.

I ran after him. I figured it would be much better if we were at least lost together.

We stopped at the first exhibit we came to, but there was no IST person in sight. Forty wax dummies stood behind a red velvet rope. Each dummy had a numbered sign at his feet. A panel at the top read:

DIAL-A-PRESIDENT

PRESS A BUTTON AND HEAR
ACTUAL QUOTES FROM
THE PRESIDENT OF YOUR CHOICE.

"Look, Fawn," said Craig. "This is neat!"

"Come *on*, Craig," I urged. I looked around for an IST worker.

"I WOULD SOONER BE A CONSTABLE THAN RUN FOR PRESIDENT. DID YOU KNOW THAT I WAS THE SMALLEST PRESIDENT? I WEIGHED 100 POUNDS. I AM JAMES MADISON."

I couldn't believe it! Craig was fooling around.

"MY NAME IS RUTHERFORD B. HAYES. NO ONE EVER LEFT THE PRESIDENCY WITH MORE REGRET."

"Gee!" said Craig, "I wonder why?"

Impatiently I said, "I don't know, but I've never stayed in one place with more regret. Come on, we've *got* to find the lobby!"

Craig pushed the button for Herbert Hoover. A light shone on a president in a gray suit.

"PROSPERITY IS JUST AROUND THE COR- NER. I WAS BORN IN A SMALL TOWN IN IOWA. I WENT TO SCHOOL AT . . . "

43

I couldn't take it anymore. Where was the lobby? Where was an IST helper? How much trouble were we in? Why did Craig have to listen to every president there was?

"Come *on*, Craig!" I insisted. "Let's get help!"

I grabbed his arm and tried to get him to follow me.

"Let go!" he yelled.

I shouldn't have let go. As soon as I did, Craig lost his balance and crashed into Rutherford B. Hayes. I stared in sheer horror as Rutherford's head fell off and rolled five feet away.

Of all times, an IST helper came around the corner.

"What happened?" she exclaimed, stooping to pick up the head.

But Craig and I were running the other way.

Six

AFTER we got as far as Ye Olde Time Village, I stopped to catch my breath. Craig was leaning against an antique doll store, panting. I wanted to think that this all wasn't happening. I wanted to stroll into the shop and look at the delicate little dresses. Instead, I forced myself to think about how much trouble we were in.

Straightening up, I looked around for an IST worker. Ye Olde Time Village was built like a town from long ago. It had a brick "street" with stores and houses on both sides. Across the street I saw a sign saying "The Olde Time Village Dentist's Office." Through the window I saw a man in a white coat talking to two ladies. I walked inside the office and waited for him to finish talking.

He showed the ladies tools which dentists of long ago used. I cleared my throat and spoke up.

"Excuse me, sir, but there was a P.A. announcement telling that guy"—I pointed out the window toward Craig—"and me to meet somebody at the information booth. Could you please tell me how to get there?"

The man smiled and excused himself from the ladies. "Are you with a class?" he asked.

I nodded. Then I pulled out my orange ticket and showed it to him.

"Why don't I call the information booth for you? I'll bet your teacher is worried!" he said.

I *knew* that Ms. Angelvine was worried. I wondered if I had embarrassed her in front of her old teacher. I wondered if Mrs. Underhill thought I was a troublemaker.

Craig joined me. Together we stood and listened to the dentist as he talked on a security phone. He said a few "uh-huhs" and a couple of "hmmms" and then turned to us.

"It seems that your class chaperone thought that it would be easier for her to find both of you here than for you two to look for the lobby. Why don't you sit here and wait? She shouldn't be but a few minutes." Smiling at us, the man gestured toward some old-fashioned chairs in his office.

"Thank you," I said. Craig said nothing. I jabbed his foot with my toe so the man wouldn't notice.

"Oh, yeah, thanks," said Craig. He gave me a dirty look.

The chairs were made of a bristly dark red material that sort of made my skin itch. Sitting there with Creepy Craig was just about the least comfortable thing I had ever done in my life.

"Maybe I'll go look at some shops while you wait here for Mrs. Underhill," Craig muttered.

I glared at him.

"I wouldn't if I were you," I suggested. "We're in enough trouble as it is."

Craig didn't say anything, but he didn't wander

off, either. He gave me another dirty look.

"Well, there you are!"

I looked up, and there was Mrs. Underhill. I couldn't believe she was actually smiling at us. I noticed that she had taken her brooch off.

"We got separated in the coal mine," Craig started to explain. "Fawn wanted to see what was around the corner. We ended up on a stage where some guy was demonstrating electricity with porcupines."

I was about to call Craig a liar but decided that Mrs. Underhill wouldn't appreciate names like that. Instead, I gave him another glare. It was the nastiest glare my face could manage.

"Hmmm," said Mrs. Underhill. "We probably learned a good lesson, didn't we?"

"Yes," said Craig and I at the same time.

Mrs. Underhill motioned for us to follow her. She began to explain, "After the class rode out of the coal mine, Bev noticed that the two of you were missing. Of course everyone was worried, and Linda kindly offered to go back to the

48

entrance and look for the two of you. The rest of the class waited and waited.

"Linda returned thinking that maybe you had both followed the tracks to where the class was. That's when your teacher asked me to have a P.A. announcement made."

We continued following her. Mrs. Underhill walked a little slowly, but I was in no hurry to join the rest of the class. We rode with her in the elevator to the third floor. When we got out she continued, "I believe the rest of the class should be in the planetarium now. They only got there ten or fifteen minutes ago."

As Mrs. Underhill opened the door to the planetarium, light entered the dark room from the hall. Sure enough, I could see some of my classmates' faces. Mrs. Underhill had one hand on Craig's shoulder and the other on mine. After the door closed, she whispered to us, "Why don't you both find seats quietly?"

"Good idea," I thought to myself. I'd do anything as long as it couldn't go wrong.

Craig sat down where he was on a step by a row of seats. I started to inch along the wall to where I thought I saw Bev.

The planetarium was in the shape of a circle. Classical violin music played in the background over an intercom. The ceiling looked like it was lit up with hundreds of stars. Linda was talking to the class about different constellations. I wished I hadn't missed anything because the planetarium was neat.

I could see the dark forms of the other kids watching the ceiling. Some kids called out their guesses for the names of constellations that Linda pointed out with a special flashlight.

I was almost to where I thought Bev was. I hoped there was someplace to sit where I wouldn't be noticed. What if the other kids were mad at me for making them wait at the coal mine?

I decided that if I wanted to survive the rest of the day, I had better stay away from Craig. All I had to do was stick my hands in my pockets, walk where the rest of the class walked, and keep my mouth glued shut.

Then I heard Linda announce, "Okay, kids, I want you to let your eyes get accustomed to the dark for a while. We're going to pretend we're in a space shuttle taking a peaceful trip around Earth. This is called a 'simulation,' and you'll be seeing our planet as an astronaut probably would."

The stars disappeared from the ceiling. The room became pitch black. None of us could even see our hands. I reached out for the wall so I could find my way to the chairs.

Suddenly I felt my hand push a lever on the wall.

Music, the kind you hear in science fiction movies when spaceships start racing, blared. Bright lights flipped on at the same time, and a man's recorded voice started thanking visitors for visiting the IST Planetarium.

When I finally opened my eyes, I saw my entire class staring at me. Of course, they automatically knew that it was my fault.

Seven

I quietly found a seat. Linda resumed taking the rest of the class on the simulated space trip. I didn't need any simulation. I was wishing so hard that I was any place but Earth that I didn't need all the special effects.

When it was time for our class to leave, Ms. Angelvine announced that she would meet Craig and me at the exit. I looked at Bev, who was sitting across the aisle. She looked back at me as if to ask, What's going *on* with you today?

I shrugged my shoulders. I looked at my feet until everyone else had filed out of the room. Then I got up to go. Craig was already standing by Ms. Angelvine. Great, I thought to myself. He's probably already blamed everything on me.

As I joined them, I noticed that Ms. Angelvine wasn't exactly in a happy mood. Her arms were crossed and she had an exasperated look on her face. At least I thought it was an exasperated look. With Ms. Angelvine, you couldn't be sure.

"Fawn and Craig," she said in a slow, careful tone, "I am exasperated with you two."

Now I was sure.

"What is *wrong* with the two of you today? How could you guys get lost like that? Do you two know how worried we've been? Fawn, do you think you can settle down and behave? Craig, *why* must you do everything Fawn tells you to do?"

I gave Craig another one of my deadly looks.

"Listen to me, you two. For the rest of the day you are to stay apart from each other. You are to both behave. You are to both make sure that you *constantly* stay by either me or Mrs. Underhill." She looked at us with the sternest look I've ever seen her give.

Craig and I stood there silently. The rest of the class had already left with Linda and Mrs. Underhill for the shadow room. I wasn't at all sure what I could say that would make Ms. Angelvine think I was a normal kid again.

Craig, however, thought of something. "Maybe Fawn and I could take turns sitting in the IST office. Then we wouldn't have to see each other."

"What!" said Ms. Angelvine with that special look of horror only teachers have. "You don't think that you are capable of behaving?"

I was pretty amazed myself at what a dopey suggestion that was. But from Craig. . . .

"I expect *common sense* from the two of you for the rest of this field trip. Am I understood?"

We both nodded.

"Okay. Now Craig, you start walking the way the class went. Fawn, you and I will be right behind. There will be *no* talking." She twisted our heads in the direction we were supposed to go.

I silently walked along beside her, trying my best to maintain a perfect three and a half foot distance to her left side. My heart was pounding pretty fast. I hardly ever got into trouble.

I decided that when we got to the shadow room I would do nothing but stand still in one place—*anyplace,* as long as it wasn't near Craig.

When the three of us joined the class, Linda had already begun talking. The shadow room had three black walls. A fourth wall had a huge greenish-white screen on it. On a table in the middle of the room was a movie camera.

Linda explained, "We've found that it is possible to store light. Normally, light travels at a very fast speed. With a chemical called 'phosphorous,' we'll be able to capture a moving shadow. Has anyone here ever seen a strobe light?"

Jim Hunt raised his hand. "Yeah . . . my big brother's high school marching band used one during a football game halftime show. It was great—it looked like an old movie or something."

"I'll bet that was neat!" said Linda. "Well, I'm going to use a strobe light to help us capture some shadows."

With that she turned on the camera, which sent light out in fast flickers. When she waved her arm up and down in front of the screen, it really did look like an old movie!

"Okay," shouted Linda, "who wants to be first? I'm going to count backward from ten, and then no matter what your motions are, I'll be able to record your shadow when I say 'freeze.'"

Bobby McDonald stepped up. He pretended like he was boxing. Although he did footwork and punches, his shadow froze into a gray color when Linda reached "freeze." It was pretty neat.

"Ooh! I have an idea!" said Jim, his hand raised high.

He whispered something into Linda's ear and then told Bobby to do the exact same thing. Again Bobby went into his boxing routine. Jim just stood there with his arms folded, humming.

But when Linda said "freeze," Jim reached out as if he were punching Bobby. We all laughed when we saw the shadow. After all the energy Bobby spent, the shadow looked as if Jim had knocked him out in a single punch.

More kids took turns. Sometimes two of them would try to do something funny together (thanks to Jim's great idea). Then Craig got up there. He announced to the class that he was going to do an imitation of Pelé, the great Brazilian soccer player. The Turkey Busters started cheering.

Craig waited as Linda counted down. At "two," he made a short run, and then he jumped up as if kicking a field goal. I had to admit it did look pretty good. His left knee bent and his right foot stretched as high as his chin. "Look at that form!" he shouted.

The Ground Hoggers booed and groaned. Betsy Mueller, the goalie on my team, said, "Come on, captain!"

I shook my head. I had promised myself that I would stand still.

Some of the Turkey Busters snickered. "The captain of the Hogs is a chicken!" I heard someone say. More laughter.

I looked at the faces of some of the Ground Hoggers. Then I thought, Why not? The worst that could happen would be for me to fall flat on my bottom. Maybe I could do a better soccer kick than Craig. That would impress everyone.

As I neared the screen, the Ground Hoggers started cheering. After all the rotten things that had happened, I felt good when I heard that. "Ready," I informed Linda. As she neared "three," I backed a few feet and then started to jump as high as I could.

But then I heard someone scream "Aaaagh!" And Linda yelled, "Freeze."

I landed and turned to look at everyone. I noticed that the Turkey Busters were hysterical. The Ground Hoggers rolled their eyes and shook their heads. I didn't want to look at the screen. But when I saw Craig laughing his head off, I had to look.

My shadow looked ridiculous. My feet looked like blocks. But what was weird was that my arms and legs were all over the place. I looked more like a broken doll than a great soccer player.

Eight

THE next stop for our class was a brief visit to the model train room. Then we would get to eat lunch, which was a good thing because I was starving.

As we entered the room, Linda told us that the Frankfort Model Train Association sponsored this exhibit. "You're looking at one of the largest model trains in the country. There are seventy feet of track and sixty-five cars. This train is set up on what's called an 'HO scale,'" Linda continued. "This exhibit is many classes' favorite." She waved across the room at a man dressed in denim overalls and an engineer's cap.

As our class gathered around the layout, the

man pulled a lever on a box he held in his hand. A little train whistled and chugged, then appeared from behind a hill. As I watched, he pressed a red button.

Clang! Clang! Clang!

A bell sounded and the train stopped beside a little station. Plastic people no bigger than my little finger held suitcases. They waited on the platform beside the track. Some sat on benches.

A puff of smoke burst from the engine's stack as it left the station. Again the bell clanged, and the little train picked up speed. It chugged into a countryside setting. We all pointed with delight at the many miniature things that stood waiting for the train to pass them. There were barns, animals, houses, kids playing, and even horses pausing in mid-air as they galloped beside a farmhouse.

I smiled at the peaceful setting.

Bev, next to me, said, "Wouldn't it be neat to

ride a train like that?" She grinned.

I nodded in agreement with her. If I had lived in those days, I would have been a railroad conductor. Then I could look out the train's window and see beautiful things like this.

"Fawn," asked Bev quietly, "did Ms. Angelvine get mad at you two after the planetarium show?"

I didn't answer, but nodded a silent "yes" with a grim look on my face. Good ol' Bev gave me a friendly jab in the arm and told me not to worry.

Suddenly I remembered that I had promised Ms. Angelvine that I wouldn't get close to Craig and that I would keep her or Mrs. Underhill in sight. Looking up, I saw Craig was only five feet away. Mrs. Underhill stood on the other side of the tracks, so I nudged Bev's arm and said, "Let's go over there."

Other IST visitors had joined our class, so Bev and I had to weave our way to the other side.

"What's going on?" asked Bev.

"Ms. Angelvine told Craig and me to stay away from each other. We each have to stick with her or Mrs. Underhill, too." I looked at Bev wistfully. "I'll just die if I get into any more trouble today."

Just then Ms. Angelvine announced, "Okay, class, we'll be going to the cafeteria now. Does everybody have their lunch tickets?"

Bev and I checked our pockets and pulled out our orange tickets.

"Good," said Ms. Angelvine. "I'd like to have a line of girls here and a line of boys here. We'll stop at the restrooms on our way to eat."

Quickly Bev and I lined up with the other girls. I began to have hope that the rest of the day might be fine. But then I felt a quick tug at my hands, and looked down in horror. I realized someone had grabbed my lunch ticket.

I didn't have to look up to know who it was. With a sinister look on his creepy face, Creepy Craig was making his way to the end of the boys' line.

Great, I thought. Oh, well. I'll just tell Ms. Angelvine or Mrs. Underhill when I see them. I knew I didn't have to react to Craig's stupid tricks. I'd just wait patiently for a teacher.

Linda waved good-bye to us and said she'd see us again when we got to the Zoo Room.

As our lines headed out, I turned to take one last look at the whistling train. That's when an uneasy feeling came over me. Just as the train's engine disappeared into a forest of pines, I noticed a little orange thing sticking out of a black coal car.

Craig, you jerk! I thought. Despite my promise, I went back to the end of the girls' line. Craig snickered.

While everyone else filed out, I stayed and watched the train make its round. I quickly ran over to where the train would soon be, and waited for my ticket to pass. As I reached for the orange ticket, I knocked over one of the other coal cars. With my ticket in my hand, I watched in misery as the back half of the train fell off the track.

In two seconds the guy in overalls was right there. He looked at me and asked me what I was doing. I just looked at the stupid ticket in my hand. I couldn't even speak. The man went on for another minute or two about how expensive the exhibit was and the signs I should have read about not touching anything.

After mumbling an apology, I scuttled out the door to catch up with the rest of my class.

"Fawn Forrester." Ms. Angelvine had her arms crossed again. This time she was tapping her foot.

"Yes, ma'am," I said.

"When you finish using the restroom, you are to meet me right here at this exact spot. Do you understand, young lady?"

"Yes, ma'am," I said again.

All the other girls hushed up as soon as I entered the restroom.

"Boy are *you* in trouble," offered Betsy Mueller.

"Yeah," said someone else.

"You're making Ms. Angelvine mad at everyone, Fawn—just because you keep getting

separated." Nancy Nelson looked at me like I was the world's worst criminal.

"You guys," piped in Bev, "Craig grabbed her ticket. Craig's the one who's been getting Fawn in trouble all day. Take it easy on her!"

I gave Bev a grateful look. Washing my hands in silence, I didn't tell anyone about knocking over the train. I just didn't have the heart to.

Nobody spoke to me. I went over and whispered to Bev to eat with the others because I'd be glued to Ms. Angelvine for the rest of the day.

When I left the restroom, I felt like crying. Why did Craig always pick on me? Everything was going wrong, and none of it was my fault! Well, maybe some things were. But I was the only one getting in trouble.

I didn't want to tell on Craig because if Ms. Angelvine didn't believe me, I knew I'd cry for sure. Besides, then I'd have to mention the train crash. I didn't want to do that, so I silently stood next to Ms. Angelvine and just hung my head.

It was awful. Everywhere Ms. Angelvine went, I

had to walk right next to her. All I needed was a leash. We entered the IST cafeteria, and everyone handed their tickets to a cafeteria aide. We sat down at some long tables, and more aides handed out boxed lunches and milk.

I sulked next to Ms. Angelvine as she and Mrs. Underhill talked about differences in teaching these days. Everyone ignored me. It was all I could do to swallow any food. I didn't even touch my hamburger.

Across the room, Craig and his friends were laughing and playing with their food. He saw me watching him, and took two pickles out of his hamburger. Then he held one up to each eye and gave me a nerdy smile.

Quickly glancing to make sure I wouldn't get caught, I stuck my tongue out at him. I heard Mrs. Underhill clear her throat and realized that she had seen me.

I closed up my lunchbox, put my elbows on the table, and put my head in my hands. Then I opened my lunchbox and counted the sesame seeds on my hamburger bun.

When I got up to seventy-nine seeds, Ms. Angelvine stood and announced, "Listen up, everyone. Clean up your area. Then line up girls and boys again, just like before."

Turning to me, she added, "And *you* stay right next to me."

Nine

OUR class took the elevators up to the fourth floor where the Twenty-first Century Exhibit was located. I stood next to Ms. Angelvine, watching everyone else go up in groups. They were laughing, talking, and having a good time. As the last load got on to go up to where Mrs. Underhill waited with the others, Ms. Angelvine placed her arm on my shoulder and guided me on board.

"Is everyone having a good time?" she asked.

"Yeah!" all the kids shouted. I didn't say anything.

"Fawn," said Ms. Angelvine, looking down at me, "you're not having the best day are you?"

I wanted to say I was having the worst. Instead, I just sort of glumly shook my head. As we climbed floors, I tried multiplying nine years times 365 days. That was it. Out of at least 3,285 days, this was the worst day of my existence. This day was a disaster.

The Twenty-first Century Exhibit was super-fascinating. One section featured computers that responded to voices. Mrs. Underhill was really amazed at those. Turning to Ms. Angelvine and me, she joked. "All I ever wanted were kids who would respond to my voice."

We laughed, and then my teacher and I walked over to look at wall charts predicting the design of a space station. "Maybe you'll get a job on something like that someday!" suggested Ms. Angelvine with a smile. It was nice to be smiled at again.

Next to the space station charts was a big plastic ball with water and plants in it. I asked Ms. Angelvine if I could go look at it. The sign that described the ball said, "An Ecosphere—

bacteria, algae, and shrimp are contained without any other source of food. Current experiments with ecospheres and biospheres may someday help establish a colony on Mars."

"Wow!" I exclaimed. "I wonder if I'll ever get to go to Mars?"

Mrs. Underhill joined us. "I remember when Charles Lindbergh flew across the Atlantic . . . to think that I also saw man walk on the moon!"

Other kids in the class came over. We moved to a large, clear tub containing water. Tomatoes were growing in it—but there wasn't any soil!

"How can tomatoes grow just in water?" asked Steve Munroe.

Jim Hunt read the sign that described the tub. "Hydroponics—farming without soil. Water, light, and nutrition are the only requirements of plants. If water is mixed with the proper nutrients, plants can be grown in special greenhouses, revolutionizing farming techniques. Hydroponics may someday play a role in the self-survival of space colonies. When these tomatoes ripen, they are used in the IST cafeteria's salad bar."

I looked around for Bev and noticed that a lot of kids were gathered around a small black room. I asked Ms. Angelvine if she would mind if we went over there. She wanted to stay at the hydroponics exhibit, so Mrs. Underhill offered to accompany me.

The room that so many of my classmates were attracted to was the holography exhibit. Mrs. Underhill and I craned our necks to see what the others were so excited about. When it was my turn to step into the little dark room, I saw some projectors attached to the walls. In the middle of the room was a projection of a banana, but it had three dimensions to it! It looked exactly like a real banana, bruises and all. I could run my hand through the image, and when I walked around the room I could even see different angles! That, I thought to myself, is just too cool.

Ms. Angelvine clapped her hands and called for everyone to meet her at a little stage area. I wondered if some other poor soul was going to be a porcupine guinea pig.

Suddenly, a shiny object that looked like a computerized trash can rolled across the stage. Making a whirring noise, it turned and faced us.

"HELLO. HOW ARE YOU TODAY? MY NAME IS BINKO. I AM A ROBOT. I AM ONE YEAR OLD. I KNOW MORE THAN MOST LIBRARIES. WOULD SOMEONE LIKE TO ASK ME WHAT THE CAPITAL OF ANY COUNTRY IS?"

The robot twisted its head completely around five times. We laughed at it.

Jim raised his hand and asked, "What's the capital of Iceland?"

"REYKJAVIK. THAT'S EASY."

Then a scientist dressed in a white IST uniform joined Binko on stage and apologized for the robot's manner. "Binko thinks that the more you know, the better a robot you are. Don't you Binko?"

"OF COURSE," was Binko's reply. Again he turned his head around a few times.

The scientist went on and explained that he actually answered Jim's question to Binko by using controls offstage. He then asked Binko to leave the stage.

Binko shook his head no. We all laughed.

Then, slapping his forehead as if he had forgotten something, the scientist asked Binko to leave *please*. Binko's head spun around a few times, and he rolled offstage with lights flashing. We all waved good-bye to the little robot, and then watched a film about different types of robots.

We eventually left the Twenty-first Century area and entered a big space called "Experimentation." There we found all sorts of booths, exhibits, and mini-centers which we were free to examine.

Everybody but me, of course. I kept alternating between Mrs. Underhill and Ms. Angelvine. I looked at a clock and realized that it had been at least a full hour since anything disastrous had happened. Then it occurred to me that for the same amount of time I hadn't even seen Creepy

Craig. No wonder things were going so well.

"Hey, Fawn," said a voice I didn't want to hear. "Look at this!"

I looked instead at Ms. Angelvine.

"Craig," said the teacher. "Remember what I said about you and Fawn."

Some of the kids in the class started giggling. "What about him and Fawn?" asked Nancy.

"Yeah," added Bobby, "weren't they kissing in the coal mine?"

"*Barf-ola!*" I cried.

"Gag me with a dead fish," grumbled Craig. Then he stalked away.

I felt my cheeks burning as I accompanied Ms. Angelvine to an exhibit called "Jacob's Ladder." It was just two metal rods that were wider at the top than the bottom. I pressed a yellow button, and suddenly blue sparks of electricity crawled up to the top, arching from one pole to the other. It looked like something out of a mad scientist's laboratory.

Other kids came over to try Jacob's Ladder,

too. Bobby thought he'd be funny, but he was only being a jerk. "This is what happens between Fawn and Craig when they stand near each other!" Luckily nobody laughed. I felt pretty confident that the world knew I couldn't stomach Craig Fuller.

Then Ms. Angelvine and I walked over to a table with all sorts of magnets on them. I picked up a heavy metal magnet with a red top. While I was looking at it, all of a sudden I found my magnet attached to a magnet held by Craig.

"I didn't know he was near me!" I said to Ms. Angelvine.

Ms. Angelvine sighed. Then she said, "Why don't you two just pull apart your magnets and find different places to be, okay?"

That was easier said than done. Our magnets were really heavy—and really stuck. Betsy Mueller, who was standing nearby, grabbed onto my waist and started pulling, too. Then Jim Hunt grabbed Craig's waist. Before we knew it, about half of the class was pulling on either Craig's side

of the magnet war or mine.

"Children!" cried Ms. Angelvine.

Craig suddenly let go of his entire magnet, and my side went tumbling down on top of each other. I cried "*Ouch!*" as the magnets landed on my left foot.

"How do you two manage it?" asked Ms. Angelvine. "Craig . . . get away from Fawn, NOW!"

I couldn't believe it. For once Craig got the blame for causing trouble. I smirked.

"Fawn! *Why* must you always tangle with Craig?"

My smile faded. I knew that it wouldn't do any good to try explaining to Ms. Angelvine. Anyway, I wondered why myself.

Ten

THE Zoo Room was our last stop for the day. As I walked at the front of the girls' line with Ms. Angelvine, I heard her mutter something about going to the zoo next year with ten chaperones.

Inside, the room was alive with animal sounds—cheeps, whistles, barks, and squawks.

The first thing we saw was a glass case filled with spiders. Their little legs crept up and down branches. I shuddered. Spiders were as gross as snakes and worms.

Linda walked up to our class. She looked refreshed and rested—probably because she got a break from me, the Disaster Kid.

"Don't worry, there's no need to be afraid of most spiders," she said. "Did you know that spiders are very nearsighted? They can only see a few inches in front of them. They also can't run very far, either. Spiders get tired easily."

I looked more closely at the spiders. They didn't seem so gross anymore.

Inside the next case we saw what seemed to be only leaves and branches from a tree.

"This one must be empty," I said, peering through the glass. Other kids looked inside, too, and agreed with me.

"Look more closely," urged Linda. "Let me know who's first to see something."

Bev cried, "I see them!"

"Where?" the rest of us asked. Then suddenly I saw them, too. Hanging underneath the branches were green caterpillars.

Linda explained, "These are spicebush swallowtail caterpillars. When they hang upside down like that they're very hard to see. That's their defense against being eaten by birds. Watch what happens when I put this caterpillar on *top* of the branch."

With that, Linda opened a screen covering the case and placed a reluctant caterpillar on top of a branch. The little thing immediately scurried down until it was back on the bottom.

"Hey, everybody! These rats are playing basketball!" It was Craig's voice from across the room. I wanted to go over and look, so I looked at Ms. Angelvine with pleading eyes.

"Oh, go ahead," she said with a warning look. She went over to where Mrs. Underhill was sitting in a chair. Mrs. Underhill looked a little tired.

A white rat was inside a cage. He held a little metal ball in his mouth. It was the size of a marble. The bottom of the cage was painted to look like a basketball court. The rat ran across the court with the ball in his mouth. Then he stood up on his hind legs and dropped the ball through a metal hoop. As the ball fell, a little window opened in the side wall. He ran over, stuck his head in, and pulled out a piece of food. Then he nibbled on it.

When the food was all gone, the rat picked up his "basketball" again. He ran with it to the net and repeated the same thing all over.

"Double dribble!" I called out. Some kids giggled.

"Hey, Fawn, maybe you could use him on your soccer team. Then you could call yourselves the 'Ground Rats.'"

I turned up my nose to let Craig know that I was not amused. But then I couldn't resist it. "Then there would be at least one rat on each team."

My Ground Hoggers laughed. I glanced over my shoulder and saw that Ms. Angelvine was still talking to Mrs. Underhill. I got away with cracking on Craig! What was even better, he couldn't come up fast enough with a reply.

I moved away from the rat cage.

PEEP! PEEP! CHEEP! PEEP!

"Look, Bev," I said. "Baby chicks!"

We ran over to a long board covered with cages. In each cage was a group of baby chicks. They were so cute!

Linda came over to explain some things about the chicks to us. "See?" she said. "On each cage is a sign that tells you how old the chickens are. These are three days old. These are two days old. And these are one day old."

"I like the one-day-old ones the best!" I exclaimed.

They looked like little balls of the softest yellow fluff. Even the tiny noises they made were cute!

"Look at these!" exclaimed Bev.

We moved to a box next to the one-day-old cage. The box was filled with eggs.

"I guess these are zero days old," I said. No sooner had I uttered those words than a little crack appeared in one of the eggs. "Look, Ms. Angelvine!" I shouted. "This egg is hatching!"

Both Ms. Angelvine and Mrs. Underhill came over to join our observation. "Class! Class! Come over here! We get to see a baby chick being born!" Ms. Angelvine said.

At Ms. Angelvine's words, everyone left the basketball-playing rat. They rushed over to where Bev and I stood beside the box of eggs.

The crack cracked open more. A little yellow beak appeared. It kept pecking at the hole. After a while a damp, yellow head poked through the top of the egg. Little dark eyes stared at a new world. The beak opened up, and the baby chick's first peep came squeaking out.

The baby chick squeezed and wiggled its shoulders through the egg hole. Then it pushed some more. At last it fell completely out of the egg. The new little chick lay on its side, peeping.

Linda asked that we not touch the new chick. "But," she added, "there are some older chicks that two students at a time can handle— carefully."

Everyone was excited. Bev and I waited for our turn together. We watched as Linda carefully handed out darling little chicks to two people at a time. When our turn finally came, I held a soft and warm chick that I immediately fell in love with. It felt like a wiggling powder puff.

Suddenly everyone heard Mrs. Underhill exclaim, "Oh, dear!"

She had a worried look on her face, and her fingers patted her dress collar searching for her brooch.

"What's wrong?" asked Ms. Angelvine.

"My brooch! It's missing!" Mrs. Underhill said in an alarmed voice.

Ms. Angelvine gazed hopefully around the Zoo Room. "Can everyone help check around for Mrs. Underhill's butterfly pin?"

Carefully we all started searching high and low. Linda offered to call the security office on the telephone intercom. "Then," she explained, "if anyone else finds it, the security force will know who it belongs to."

I went to the chicken cage and put my baby chick back. Then I joined everyone else in the search.

Everyone checked somewhere. I was helping Bev look underneath cages, when suddenly I heard Linda scream "EEEK!"

I looked up to see what her problem was. There were baby chicks all over the place! And then I slapped my forehead. I had forgotten to close the cage door when I put my little chick back!

About twenty baby chicks were loose. Little puffs of yellow hopped this way and that. They had run out of their cage and were skittering across the floor.

One chick hopped beside the fish tank. One ran right through Ms. Angelvine's feet. She turned, scooped it up, and put it back in its cage. She looked at me as she latched shut the door.

Linda snatched a chick from underneath the gopher cage.

"I forgot to latch the cage," I uttered.

"Way to go, Fawn," said Julie Johnson. "Can't you do *anything* right today?"

Craig stared at me. "Why'd you let all the

chickens go? You're so—"

"Craig!" screamed Ms. Angelvine. "Leave Fawn alone."

Everyone was scrambling somewhere. I just stood there, too shocked to join in the hunt for either baby chicks or the butterfly pin.

Finally, Linda announced that all the chicks were back in the cage. But no one had seen anything of Mrs. Underhill's brooch.

Disappointed, Ms. Angelvine looked at her watch. "We may not be able to find it, kids." She gave Mrs. Underhill a sympathetic look. "And that was so special of you to wear that today," she said to her old teacher.

I wondered what she meant by that.

Eleven

MRS. Underhill sighed. "I'm sure it will turn up someday. But I have to say that it would be such a disappointment to lose that after all these years!"

I think we all felt pretty sorry for Mrs. Underhill, especially me. She had been so nice to me, in spite of my disasters. I wished there was something I could do to find or replace her brooch.

"Okay, kids," said Ms. Angelvine with a tired sigh. "Our bus driver is supposed to meet us at the front door in fifteen minutes. That just gives us enough time to make it to the lobby. Are there any emergency restroom requests?"

Two kids had to go. The rest of us lined up to ride the elevators back down to the lobby. I wasn't sure I wanted to go back there. I'd have to look at the four thousand dominoes I had massacred.

Before we got on the elevators, everyone thanked Linda. I timidly mumbled a special thank you that I really meant. She smiled and said, "You're all very welcome. We hope you'll come visit us again at IST."

I wasn't sure by the tone of her voice whether she really meant that. After today, I thought, she'd probably look for a new job.

When we arrived back at the lobby, I noticed sadly that the entire domino exhibit had been cleaned up. I wondered if the kids from Douglas Alternative were even going to bother redoing it.

I watched Mrs. Underhill as she checked a final time with the security office. When she turned back with a sad look on her face, I knew they hadn't found her pin.

Suddenly something hit me. Of course! Why

hadn't I thought of that before?

I didn't want to tell Ms. Angelvine what I thought. I wasn't sure, for one thing. But I knew that she would never agree to letting me go down to the coal mine again. Especially not by myself. The other kids were milling around in the lobby, examining things and chatting. Quickly I looked for a clock. When I couldn't find one, I asked Jim Murphy if he had the time. We had less than ten minutes until we were supposed to get on the bus.

I closed my eyes and tried to think. Would it be wrong to try to get the pin? Should I tell Ms. Angelvine? Time was passing. I was afraid that Ms. Angelvine would get mad at me if I asked her. And the look on Mrs. Underhill's face. . . .

I silently sneaked away from my class. Just as I squeezed through the lobby doors that led to the coal mine, I noticed that someone was following me. Oh, please, no, I thought.

It was.

"Where do you think *you're* going?" asked

Craig. He was hurrying to catch up with me.

"Go away!" I hissed.

"Where are you going?" he demanded.

"I think I know where Mrs. Underhill's pin is."

I was surprised to see Craig's face light up. "Where?" he asked.

"I have to hurry," was all I said as I sprinted toward the stairs leading to the mine.

Maybe he would follow. But I didn't care. Craig or no Craig, I was going to get that pin for Mrs. Underhill. Clopping footsteps behind me told me that Craig was coming along. But I kept going.

I practically flew down the stairwell. I kept thinking of the school bus leaving without us. We had to hurry!

"Wait up!" panted Craig.

Soon we were both at the place where the lamp helmets were. Quickly we both grabbed one and flicked on the lights. I tried to remember . . . was it here? Where had I seen that sparkle?

Wait! I saw it from the corner when we watched the man cars trail off. "Craig!" I practically shouted. "Remember when Mrs. Underhill came to get us at the dentist's office?"

"Yeah—so why are we here if you think she left it there?"

"I think she lost it down here!" I said. I ran to what I thought was the spot where Craig and I had stood. "I noticed in the dentist's place that her brooch was missing. I figured she just took it off. But the only place we had really been between then and when she showed it to everyone was here! Also," I said, desperately trying to find the sparkle I had seen with my light, "I remember seeing a sparkle on the ground after we saw the man cars leaving."

No luck. I was ready to panic, now. Surely it had been more than ten minutes since Craig caught me sneaking out. What if I didn't find the brooch? Then I would not only not be a hero, but I would make the entire class late in getting on the bus. Or worse!

"EUREKA!" I shouted. I practically skipped over to where I saw the sparkle. Craig was right

behind me. But the tunnel was so dark that once I got to where I thought it was, I couldn't see it anymore. That's when Craig suddenly stooped over. I looked where he was stooping. There it was! The butterfly pin!

"I found it!" cried Craig. "I'm a hero!"

But I dove for it before he could pick it up. "Sorry, creep, but I'm the one who found it."

Craig kicked it with his foot before I could get my hands on it. He also kicked coal dust in my face. I grabbed some of the dust from inside the tracks and threw it at him. I wasn't about to let Craig ruin things now.

Then I scrambled to where he kicked the pin. I had it!

"I found it!" he shouted.

"Did not!" I shouted back.

"Did too!" he yelled. He grabbed it from my hand.

"Give it to me, you animal!" I screamed.

"HEY!! WHAT IS GOING ON DOWN HERE?"

Twelve

WE froze. Then I quickly grabbed the now dirty brooch back from Craig. Linda came down the stairs.

She shone a flashlight on our faces. Her jaw dropped when she realized who we were.

"Are you two planning to move in down here?" she asked.

Craig and I both started to explain at once.

"I found Mrs. Underhill's pin—" Craig began.

"I came to look for Mrs. Underhill's—" I said at the same time.

We stopped and gave each other dirty looks. Again, we both started talking at once. "It was my idea . . ." I started.

"I tried to get Fawn to go back . . ." Craig was saying.

Linda didn't understand a single thing from either of us. She rolled her eyes and pulled a pocket pager out of her coat. "Please return the man cars to the coal mine. Please return the man cars to the coal mine." She flicked her pager off, then sat down on the steps.

"Now," she began, "*I'm* going to relax. I would like to hear what Craig has to say first. I would then like to listen to Fawn. Why are you two here again, and what are you fighting and screaming about?"

Craig spoke. "I saw Fawn leave our class when we were all supposed to be waiting in the lobby. I followed her down here and just *happened* to find Mrs. Underhill's butterfly pin." Then he looked at me as if he were an injured puppy. "Then Fawn started throwing coal dust at me. She wanted to get all the credit for finding the pin."

"Oh," was all Linda said.

It was my turn, now. I looked at Linda. She

looked at me. I looked at Craig. He gave me his famous nerdy smile. I looked at the brooch in my hand. Trying to dust it off a little, I decided that it didn't matter who got the credit. The important thing was that Mrs. Underhill would get her pin back.

"I just wanted to find Mrs. Underhill's pin." That was all I said. Then I went and stood by Linda to wait for the man cars.

Nobody spoke the entire ride out of the coal mine. I dreaded facing my teacher. I had a feeling that we would have to stay after class for the next three years.

When we got into a lighted area, I laughed when I looked at Craig. He was covered with black coal dust! But then I realized that I probably looked just as bad. Craig laughed at me, too.

Linda just tapped her fingers on the car she rode in and smiled. I think she knew that Craig and I would be leaving soon.

The ride came to an end. It was kind of fun. I

found out what we missed the first time we were down in the mine. Linda quietly led Craig and me back to the lobby. Walking through those doors was not going to be fun.

Ms. Angelvine stared at us as we made our entrance. Our entire class was sitting on the floor, clutching sweaters or souvenirs they had bought.

Nobody looked happy at all.

"You guys ruin everything!" It was Bobby who said that.

"Yeah," growled some others.

Ms. Angelvine sighed deeply. "I've worried more about you two today than I've worried about all my students in the past year," she said. "Getting lost once is enough. But getting lost twice? Why are you both filthy dirty? Why did you leave? Why . . . ?" She looked too tired to go on.

"I'm sorry," I mumbled. "I thought I could find Mrs. Underhill's pin."

"I'm sorry, too," said Craig. "I went along to help her."

Ms. Angelvine held two slips of pink paper in her hand. Waving them at Craig and me, she informed us, "These slips contain reports from two—*two*—IST workers about exhibits that were harmed. Why wasn't I told about these?"

I never saw Ms. Angelvine look so disappointed. I opened my mouth to explain what happened, but she continued. "The rest of the class was forced to wait two times for you today. I think that you both, Fawn and Craig, will need to stay after school tomorrow so we can talk about how to behave."

I just looked at Craig.

"And," she continued, "I feel that you both owe the rest of the class a pretty big apology."

Together Craig and I said, "Sorry."

"I should think so. Fortunately, the bus hasn't arrived here yet. I'm going to step outside and check on it," said Ms. Angelvine. "Everyone wait here. *Don't* wander off." She glared at Craig and me with that last warning.

She strode across the lobby and out the front

door. There was silence for a minute.

"Boy, are you guys in trouble," said Diane Arps finally.

"Yeah. Ms. Angelvine said there's no way we can do a project for the lobby now," muttered Jim. Then he added, "Thanks to you."

"Ms. Angelvine said that the rest of us might want to choose new captains for the soccer game, too," said Betsy Mueller. "Captains are supposed to be *mature*."

Then Bev spoke up. "Listen, you guys, can't you see they feel bad enough?"

Everybody was silent again.

Linda looked at all of us with a raised eyebrow. "Excuse me, but I have to be going. Have a safe journey home. Bye kids!"

We all waved good-bye to her.

That was when Mrs. Underhill noticed the brooch. "My pin! You *did* find it! Oh, my heavens!" She came toward me and took the pin, looking at it as if it were the most precious thing in the world. Maybe it was . . . to her.

"Where did you find it?" everyone asked. Then suddenly the entire class came back to life, and people were smiling again.

"Fawn found it in the coal tunnel. She remembered seeing something sparkle and glitter when we were lost this morning," Craig said quietly.

I couldn't believe my ears. Craig Fuller had said something nice about me.

"It was kind of an accident," I said.

"A *good* accident," added Craig.

"Well, Fawn has certainly had her share of accidents today," said Mrs. Underhill. "I am so grateful to you for finding it." She smiled directly at me. "You know, this is a very special piece of jewelry to me."

I felt her hand on my shoulder. As she pinned the brooch back onto her collar, she continued. "I once had a class that . . . oh, let's say that it kept me on my toes," Mrs. Underhill began. "One student in particular seemed to have one disaster after another."

She blinked her eyes and put her other hand

on Craig's shoulder. "This student was a girl, and a bright one at that. But she liked to compete with a particular boy in the class. They always had to outdo each other, it seemed. One day, when our class was having its spring picnic, the two managed to get lost together. The Simmons' police, fire department and—goodness gracious —the *mayor* helped in the big search." Mrs. Underhill chuckled.

"Where were they?" we all asked eagerly.

"Well, these two wanted to see who could run the fastest. By the time they finished racing each other, they were about two miles away from the schoolgrounds. I believe they went as far as the MacIntosh farmhouse."

"That's my grandpa and grandma's place!" said Megan MacIntosh.

"How about that?" remarked Mrs. Underhill, smiling. "Anyway, they stopped in the farmhouse to call us. But no one was in the school. Everyone was out looking for the lost children! Our picnic was a catastrophe!"

"So how did you get the brooch?" I asked.

"Well," said Mrs. Underhill, "it seems that this girl felt pretty bad about ruining the picnic—in addition to a few other mistakes that year. When school ended for summer vacation, she gave me this brooch as a gift. She also wrote a nice note with it."

"What was in the note?" asked Craig.

"It was a thank-you note. Sarah thanked me for being a nice teacher. She also said that she would try to be a little more thoughtful when doing things."

"Hey!" I cried. "Isn't 'Sarah' Ms. Angelvine's first name?"

"Yeah!" everyone said.

"It most certainly is!" said Ms. Angelvine. She had come in from outside and was standing behind all of us.

I turned around, put my hands on my hips, and laughed. "You mean I'm not the worst fourth-grade disaster ever?" I asked.

"No, Fawn, I'm sorry. In fact," she said, winking at Mrs. Underhill, "you don't even come close to being the worst disaster."

After we all had a good laugh, Ms. Angelvine and Mrs. Underhill hugged good-bye. Everyone thanked Mrs. Underhill over and over as she left to go to the parking lot.

"Is everyone ready to go home?" asked our teacher.

"Yes!" we all shouted. I think that I must have shouted the loudest. After a day of chicken-chasing, magnet-wrestling, train-wrecking, dummy-breaking, porcupine-imitating, coal-shoveling, and domino-flattening, I was more than ready to get back to Simmons.

Bev and I sat together, and this time I let *her* have the window seat.

While most of the kids chattered about the trip, I just rested quietly. I thought about the day's events. I thought about being ousted as Ground Hoggers' captain. Then I thought about finding Mrs. Underhill's brooch. Even though so many things had gone wrong, finding that brooch

was something I could honestly feel great about.

And then an idea occurred to me. Maybe I'll do something nice for Ms. Angelvine. Maybe I'll give her a little present with a thank-you note, too. Who knows—twenty years from now another fourth-grade disaster queen can find whatever it is. And *sort of* be a heroine. Like me!

About the Author

As a young girl, JANET ADELE BLOSS slept with books under her pillow. She thought the characters and adventures would creep into her dreaming brain at night. She admits it never worked, but it was a nice way to fall asleep.

While growing up, Janet lived in Tennessee, Illinois, England, Switzerland, and Virginia. These moves provided her with a lot of experiences to draw upon for writing.

As early as fifth grade, Janet knew she wanted to become an author. She also wanted to be a flamenco dancer, a skater for roller derby, and a beach bum in California. But fortunately for her (and for her readers) it was the dream of becoming an author that came true.

In addition to writing, Janet had worked as a secretary, an illustrator, a map folder, a restaurant reviewer, and a manure shoveler in a horse barn.

Janet attended Kenyon College in Gambier, Ohio, where she met her husband. They live with six cats, Toby, Maully, Alicia, Winky, Wild Jaxon, and Jazz.

"I love to dance and listen to music. I also love to camp, sing, shoot pool, swim, read, play harmonica, and talk to trees. I hate lima beans."